The Tempest

William Shakespeare

SADDLEBACK
EDUCATIONAL PUBLISHING

Saddleback's *Illustrated Classics*™

SADDLEBACK
EDUCATIONAL PUBLISHING

Three Watson
Irvine, CA 92618-2767
Website: www.sdlback.com

ISBN: 1-59905-157-5

Printed in China

Welcome to Saddleback's *Illustrated Classics*™

We are proud to welcome you to Saddleback's *Illustrated Classics*™. Saddleback's *Illustrated Classics*™ was designed specifically for the classroom to introduce readers to many of the great classics in literature. Each text, written and adapted by teachers and researchers, has been edited using the Dale-Chall vocabulary system. In addition, much time and effort has been spent to ensure that these high-interest stories retain all of the excitement, intrigue, and adventure of the original books.

With these graphically *Illustrated Classics*™, you learn what happens in the story in a number of different ways. One way is by reading the words a character says. Another way is by looking at the drawings of the character. The artist can tell you what kind of person a character is and what he or she is thinking or feeling.

This series will help you to develop confidence and a sense of accomplishment as you finish each novel. The stories in Saddleback's *Illustrated Classics*™ are fun to read. And remember, fun motivates!

Overview

Everyone deserves to read the best literature our language has to offer. Saddleback's *Illustrated Classics*™ was designed to acquaint readers with the most famous stories from the world's greatest authors, while teaching essential skills. You will learn how to:

- Establish a purpose for reading
- Activate prior knowledge
- Evaluate your reading
- Listen to the language as it is written
- Extend literary and language appreciation through discussion and writing activities.

Reading is one of the most important skills you will ever learn. It provides the key to all kinds of information. By reading the *Illustrated Classics*™, you will develop confidence and the self-satisfaction that comes from accomplishment—a solid foundation for any reader.

Remember,

"Today's readers are tomorrow's leaders."

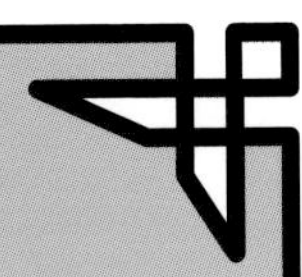

William Shakespeare

William Shakespeare was baptized on April 26, 1564, in Stratford-on-Avon, England, the third child of John Shakespeare, a well-to-do merchant, and Mary Arden, his wife. Young William probably attended the Stratford grammar school, where he learned English, Greek, and a great deal of Latin. Historians aren't sure of the exact date of Shakespeare's birth.

In 1582, Shakespeare married Anne Hathaway. By 1583 the couple had a daughter, Susanna, and two years later the twins, Hamnet and Judith. Somewhere between 1585 and 1592 Shakespeare went to London, where he became first an actor and then a playwright. His acting company, *The King's Men*, appeared most often in the *Globe* theater, a part of which Shakespeare himself owned.

In all, Shakespeare is believed to have written thirty-seven plays, several nondramatic poems, and a number of sonnets. In 1611 when he left the active life of the theater, he returned to Stratford and became a country gentleman, living in the second-largest house in town. For five years he lived a quiet life. Then, on April 23, 1616, William Shakespeare died and was buried in Trinity Church in Stratford. From his own time to the present, Shakespeare is considered one of the greatest writers of the English-speaking world.

William Shakespeare

The Tempest

ARIEL
PROSPERO
CALIBAN
MIRANDA
KING ALONSO
FERDINAND
GONZALO

THE TEMPEST* HOWLED AND HUGE WAVES THREATENED** TO SINK THE CREAKING WOODEN SHIP.
A TERRIBLE RAIN FELL FROM THE SKY. WIND RIPPED AT THE SAILS.

* storm

** warned, gave signs that something bad would happen

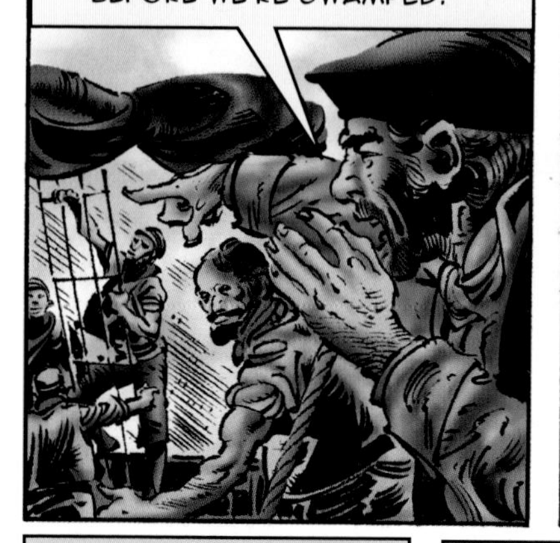
ONE OF THE SAILORS GAVE ORDERS TO TRY TO SAVE THE SHIP.
TAKE IN THOSE SAILS, MEN, BEFORE WE'RE SWAMPED.*

THE SHIP BELONGED TO KING ALONSO OF NAPLES WHO WAS RETURNING FROM A WEDDING PARTY FAR ACROSS THE SEA.
THE STORM HAD FORCED HIS SHIP FAR FROM THE OTHER BOATS IN THE FLEET.

BUT KING ALONSO TRIED NOT TO BE FRIGHTENED. HE HURRIED ACROSS THE SHIP'S DECK WITH HIS SON, PRINCE FERDINAND.

BEHIND THEM CAME SEBASTIAN, THE KING'S BROTHER, AND ANTONIO, WHO WAS THE DUKE OF MILAN.

AT THE BACK OF THE GROUP WAS WISE GONZALO, A TRUSTED ADVISOR** TO ALONSO.

* sunk by huge waves

** helper

SAILOR! I ORDER YOU TO SAVE THIS SHIP!
YOUR MAJESTY,* WE ARE DOING OUR BEST. PLEASE RETURN TO YOUR CABIN AND LET US WORK IN PEACE.

GRUMBLING THAT HE COULD NOT COMMAND THE WAVES, KING ALONSO AND HIS MEN WENT BELOW TO WAIT OUT THE STORM.

SUDDENLY, SEVERAL SAILORS BURST INTO THE ROOM. THEY WERE DRIPPING WET AND VERY TIRED.
THE SHIP IS LOST! IT WILL SOON SPLIT APART.
IF I MUST DIE, I WOULD RATHER HAVE DIED ON LAND. BUT THERE IS NOTHING WE CAN DO.

* a title for a king

MEANWHILE, JUST OUSTSIDE HIS CAVE ON A NEARBY ISLAND, THE WIZARD* PROSPERO WATCHED THE SHIP SINK.
VERY GOOD! EVERYTHING IS GOING AS I HAVE PLANNED IT.

HIS DAUGHTER, THE LOVELY MIRANDA, COULD NOT UNDERSTAND WHY HER FATHER USED HIS MAGIC TO MAKE A STORM.
FATHER, PLEASE STOP THIS TEMPEST! THAT SHIP OUT THERE HAS SANK!

I HEARD THEM CRY OUT FOR HELP. MANY LIVES WILL BE LOST!
IT IS TOO LATE NOW. BUT YOU MUST BELIEVE ME THAT NO HARM WAS DONE.

* a man who has studied magic and knows how to work with it

DEAR DAUGHTER, EVERYTHING I HAVE DONE HAS BEEN FOR YOUR GOOD!
YET YOU KNOW NOTHING OF WHO YOU ARE—AND WHO I AM—OR WAS. PERHAPS NOW IS THE TIME TO TELL YOU.
WIPE YOUR TEARS, MIRANDA, AND SIT NEXT TO ME. I WILL TELL YOU HOW WE FIRST CAME TO THIS ISLAND.

YEARS AGO, WHEN YOU WERE JUST A THREE-YEAR-OLD CHILD, I WAS THE DUKE OF MILAN.

"RUNNING THE KINGDOM BORED ME. I FOUND THAT KIND OF LIFE VERY DULL. . .!

". . .AND I LONGED TO STUDY QUIETLY IN MY PALACE LIBRARY."

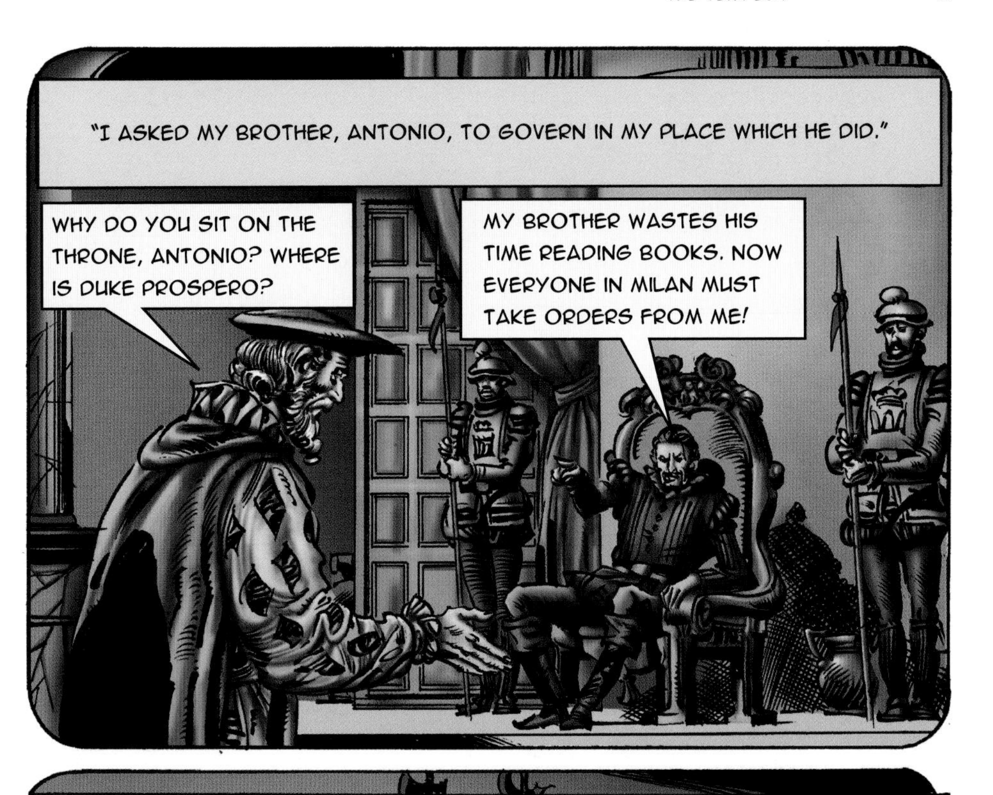
"I ASKED MY BROTHER, ANTONIO, TO GOVERN IN MY PLACE WHICH HE DID."
WHY DO YOU SIT ON THE THRONE, ANTONIO? WHERE IS DUKE PROSPERO?
MY BROTHER WASTES HIS TIME READING BOOKS. NOW EVERYONE IN MILAN MUST TAKE ORDERS FROM ME!

"AFTER A WHILE, ANTONIO DECIDED THAT HE LIKED BEING THE DUKE. HE MET SECRETLY WITH KING ALONSO OF NAPLES TO STEAL MY THRONE."
KING ALONSO, I NEED MANY OF YOUR SOLDIERS TO HELP TAKE THE THRONE OF MILAN AWAY FROM MY BROTHER PROSPERO.
I WILL HELP YOU, ANTONIO, BUT YOU MUST TAX MUCH GOLD FROM YOUR PEOPLE TO PAY FOR THE SERVICES OF MY ARMY.

"I WAS FOOLISH TO TRUST MY BROTHER TO TAKE GOOD CARE OF MILAN FOR ME. I WAS READING A BOOK ABOUT SORCERY* IN THE CASTLE LIBRARY WHEN THE GUARDS CAME TO TAKE ME AWAY."

ANTONIO AND ALONSO FROM NAPLES! GO AWAY!

WE GIVE THE ORDERS NOW, PROSPERO! GUARDS, TAKE HIM!

* magic

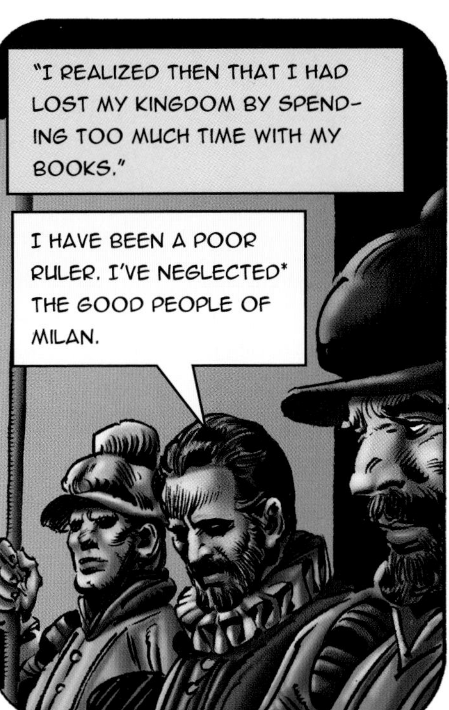
"I REALIZED THEN THAT I HAD LOST MY KINGDOM BY SPENDING TOO MUCH TIME WITH MY BOOKS."
I HAVE BEEN A POOR RULER. I'VE NEGLECTED* THE GOOD PEOPLE OF MILAN.

"MY HEART SANK EVEN MORE WHEN I SET EYES UPON YOU, MIRANDA."

MY LITTLE BABY, COME TO ME.

PAPA!

BOTH I AND MY DAUGHTER ARE AT YOUR MERCY. WHAT WILL YOU DO WITH US?
YOU SHALL SOON SEE, PROSPERO.
LET US RUSH TO THE CITY DOCKS.

"WE WERE TAKEN UNDER GUARD TO MILAN'S WATERFRONT** WHERE WE WERE PLACED ABOARD A SHIP."

* not paid enough attention to

** the place where ships load and unload their goods

"IT SAILED FOR MANY MILES, FAR FROM ANY SIGN OF LAND."

"ALONSO AND ANTONIO HAD PLOTTED THE BEST WAY TO KILL US WITHOUT LEAVING A SINGLE TRACE."
WE CANNOT KILL PROSPERO OUR-SELVES. THE PEOPLE OF MILAN STILL LOVE HIM AND WOULD TURN AGAINST US.
VERY WELL, THEN. WE WILL CAST HIM ADRIFT* AND CLAIM HE WAS LOST AT SEA.

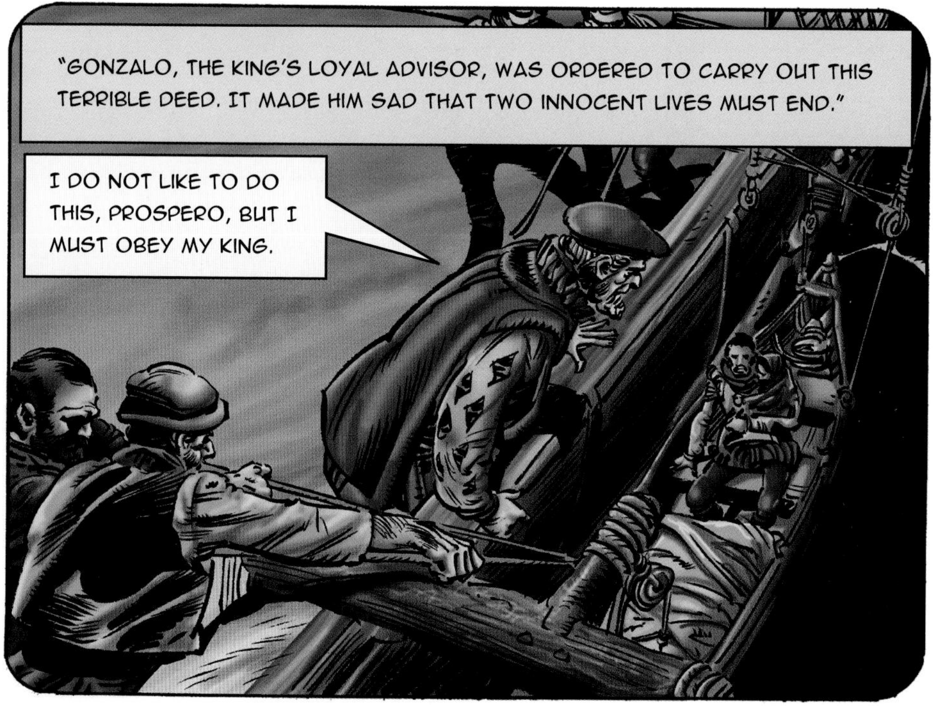
"GONZALO, THE KING'S LOYAL ADVISOR, WAS ORDERED TO CARRY OUT THIS TERRIBLE DEED. IT MADE HIM SAD THAT TWO INNOCENT LIVES MUST END."
I DO NOT LIKE TO DO THIS, PROSPERO, BUT I MUST OBEY MY KING.

* set someone in a small boat on the open sea, often without supplies

** not guilty of any crime or wrongdoing

"BUT KIND-HEARTED GONZALO HAD HIDDEN FOOD, WATER, CLOTHES, AND MANY IMPORTANT BOOKS OF MAGIC ON OUR SMALL BOAT."

BLESS GONZALO FOR THIS. OUR LIVES MAY YET BE SAVED.

"OUR LEAKING BOAT BOBBED* ON THE SEA LIKE A CORK. SOON, OUR FOOD AND WATER WERE ALMOST GONE."

"I HAD JUST ABOUT GIVEN UP HOPE WHEN WE LANDED ON THE COAST OF THIS ISLAND."
"WE FOUND A CAVE TO MAKE OUR HOME. FOR MANY MONTHS I CAREFULLY READ MY BOOKS. AND IT WAS THEN I FOUND I HAD MY MAGIC POWERS."

* moved up and down with the movement of waves

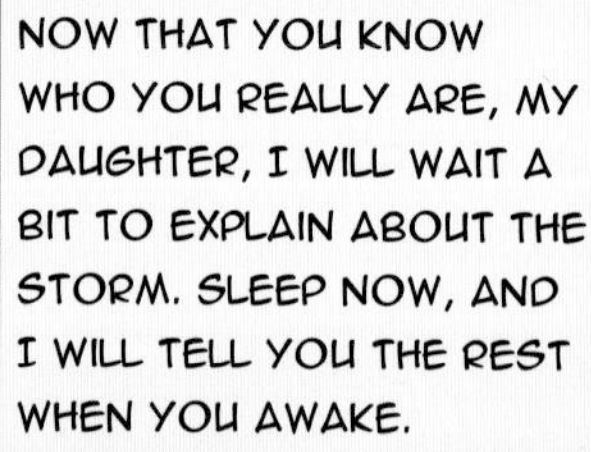

NOW THAT YOU KNOW WHO YOU REALLY ARE, MY DAUGHTER, I WILL WAIT A BIT TO EXPLAIN ABOUT THE STORM. SLEEP NOW, AND I WILL TELL YOU THE REST WHEN YOU AWAKE.

SO MIRANDA FELL ASLEEP, AND THE SPIRIT ARIEL DREW NEAR TO REPORT TO PROSPERO.

I HAVE DONE EVERYTHING YOU ORDERED ME TO DO, MASTER. WHEN THE SHIP SEEMED ABOUT TO SINK, I FLEW FROM CABIN TO CABIN AND DECK TO DECK FRIGHTENING EVERYONE.

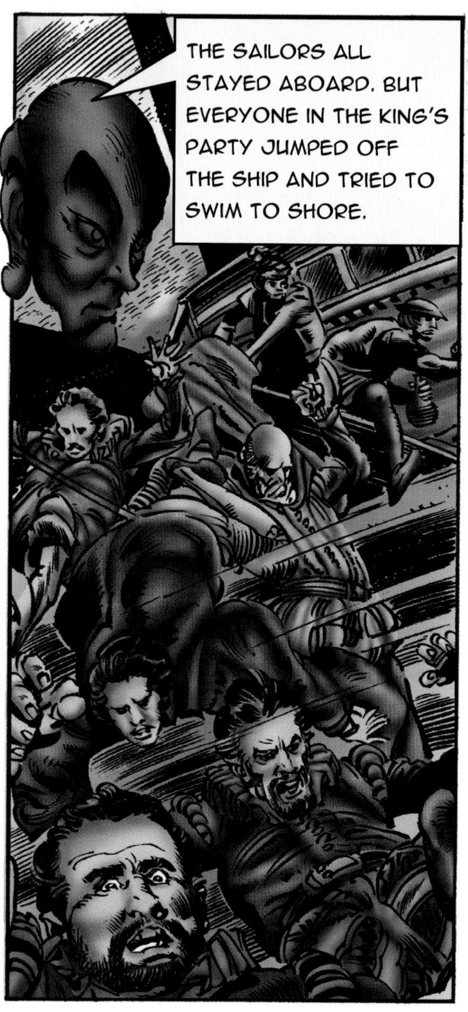
THE SAILORS ALL STAYED ABOARD. BUT EVERYONE IN THE KING'S PARTY JUMPED OFF THE SHIP AND TRIED TO SWIM TO SHORE.

"THEY ALL WENT OFF DIFFERENT DIRECTIONS, BUT EVERY ONE OF THEM IS SAFE. THEY MUST HAVE THOUGHT A DEVIL HAD TAKEN OVER THEIR SHIP!"

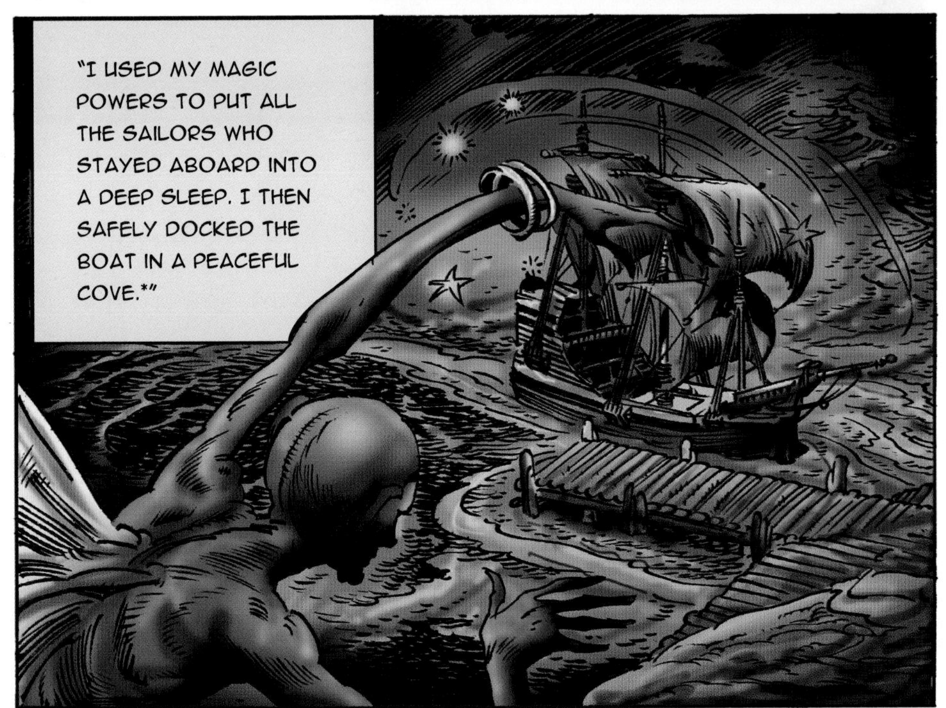
"I USED MY MAGIC POWERS TO PUT ALL THE SAILORS WHO STAYED ABOARD INTO A DEEP SLEEP. I THEN SAFELY DOCKED THE BOAT IN A PEACEFUL COVE.*"

* a small harbor

THE KING'S PARTY ARE ALL WELL SEPARATED* AND SCATTERED OVER THE ISLAND.
GOOD, ARIEL. BUT NOW I HAVE ANOTHER JOB FOR YOU.

MORE WORK, MASTER? YOU PROMISED YOU WOULD SET ME FREE!
AND I WILL, WHEN IT IS TIME. HAVE YOU FORGOTTEN HOW I RESCUED YOU FROM THE TREE IN WHICH YOU WERE IMPRISONED**?
DON'T YOU REMEM-BER THAT WITCH SYCORAX WHO WAS BROUGHT TO THIS ISLAND AND LEFT HERE? THE PEOPLE OF HER COUNTRY WERE AFRAID TO KILL HER BECAUSE OF HER MAGIC POWERS. BUT SHE HAD DONE SUCH EVIL THINGS THAT THEY HAD TO GET RID OF HER!

* kept apart from one another

** kept in a jail or other place against one's will or desires

"YOU WERE *HER* SERVANT THEN, AND YOU HATED EVERY MINUTE OF IT."

"YOU REFUSED TO OBEY HER ORDERS. SO, TO PUNISH YOU, SHE LOCKED YOU DEEP INSIDE AN OLD PINE TREE. REMEMBER, ARIEL?"
THERE YOU WILL STAY, YOU WICKED* SPIRIT, UNTIL YOU AGREE TO DO AS I SAY!
NO! NO!

"THEN SHE DIED, AND YOU WERE A PRISONER INSIDE THAT TREE FOR TWELVE YEARS! FINALLY, AS I WALKED BY ONE DAY, I HEARD YOUR CRIES AND LET YOU OUT."
I AM FREE AT LAST! OH, SIR, I WILL BE YOUR SERVANT, FOR AS LONG AS YOU WISH.

* evil

NOW ALL THAT'S LEFT OF SYCORAX IS CALIBAN, HER SON, WHO WAS BORN SHORTLY AFTER SHE ARRIVED HERE. I KEEP YOU SAFE FROM *HIM* TOO!
YES, MASTER. I WILL NOT FORGET ALL I OWE YOU. I WILL CONTINUE TO SERVE YOU WELL!

AT THAT, PROSPERO WHISPERED AN ORDER TO ARIEL, AND THE SPIRIT DEPARTED.* JUST THEN MIRANDA AWOKE.

THE STORY YOU TOLD ME WAS SO STRANGE, FATHER, THAT I COULD NOT HELP BUT FALL ASLEEP.
WELL, YOU ARE AWAKE NOW. LET US GO TO VISIT CALIBAN.

I DO NOT LIKE HIM AT ALL, FATHER.
NOR DO I. BUT HE IS USEFUL TO US, CARRYING OUR WOOD AND BUILDING OUR FIRES. THERE HE IS!

* left, went away

I SAW YOU RUN INTO YOUR CAVE, CALIBAN. COME OUT! SOME GUESTS WILL BE HERE SOON, AND WE NEED MORE WOOD FOR THE FIRE.

A CURSE* ON YOU, PROSPERO, FOR MAKING ME YOUR SLAVE!

BE QUIET, MONSTER, OR I'LL ORDER SOME SPIRITS TO PINCH YOU ALL NIGHT LONG!

YOU NEVER SPOKE TO ME LIKE THAT WHEN I WAS YOUNG! YOU WERE KIND TO ME AND GAVE ME SWEET FRUIT JUICE TO DRINK!

* evil wish

YOU TOOK ME AWAY FROM MY UGLY HOME AND BROUGHT ME TO YOUR CAVE.

"YOU TAUGHT ME THE NAMES OF THE SUN AND THE MOON—AND HOW THE SEASONS CHANGE. I LOVED YOU THEN."
BY THE TIME THE MOON IS FULL NEXT MONTH, THE BERRIES IN THE FIELDS WILL BE RIPE.

"AND BECAUSE YOU WERE GOOD TO ME, I SHOWED YOU WHERE ALL THE FRESH SPRINGS OF WATER COULD BE FOUND. I SHOWED YOU ALL THE GOOD PLACES FOR GROWING FOOD."
HERE UNDER THIS TREE FLOWS THE SWEETEST WATER ON THE ISLAND!

BUT NOW I AM SORRY I TOLD YOU THE SECRETS OF THIS PLACE. YOU HAVE BECOME ITS KING, AND I AM ONLY YOUR SLAVE!
IT WAS YOUR OWN FAULT, MONSTER! HAD YOU NOT TRIED TO ATTACK MY CHILD, THAT WOULD NOT HAVE HAPPENED!

I WAS KIND TO YOU, CALIBAN. I TAUGHT YOU TO SPEAK AND TO READ. BUT YOU WERE ALWAYS EVIL, AND NOW YOU DE-SERVE THE TREATMENT* YOU GET!

YOU COULD NOT STAY IN MY HOUSE AFTER WHAT YOU DID, AND *THAT* IS WHY YOU ARE BACK HERE. BUT ENOUGH! WE NEED MORE WOOD—GO AND GET IT!
HIS MAGIC IS POWERFUL,** AND I MUST OBEY.

* the way someone or something is handled

** strong

MEANWHILE, ARIEL HAD BECOME INVISIBLE. HE FLEW TO WHERE PRINCE FERDINAND HAD BEEN WASHED A SHORE.
I AM ALL ALONE. SURELY MY FATHER MUST HAVE DIED IN THE SEA ALONG WITH EVERYONE ELSE.
TO DRAW THE PRINCE CLOSER TO PROSPERO'S CAVE, THE SPIRIT PLAYED ON HIS FLUTE.
WHAT BEAUTIFUL SOUNDS! I MUST FOLLOW WHERE THEY LEAD ME.
ARIEL LED THE PRINCE STRAIGHT TO PROSPERO'S HOME.
THE MUSIC HAS BROUGHT ME TO A CAVE. I WONDER WHO LIVES HERE.
FERDINAND DID NOT SEE PROSPERO AND MIRANDA WATCHING HIM NEARBY.
TELL ME WHAT YOU SEE OVER THERE, MY DAUGHTER.
IT MUST BE A SPIRIT, FATHER, A VERY GOOD LOOKING SPIRIT, TOO!

* not able to be seen

EXCEPT FOR HER AGING FATHER, MIRANDA HAD NEVER SEEN ANOTHER MAN AS SHE GREW UP ON THE ISLAND.
NO, MIRANDA, HE IS A MAN. HE HAS LOST HIS FRIENDS AT SEA AND IS SEARCHING FOR THEM.
HE IS INDEED VERY NOBLE.*
CATCHING SIGHT OF MIRANDA, THE PRINCE WALKED OUT TO HER, CHARMED BY HER BEAUTY.
I AM PRINCE FERDINAND OF NAPLES.
AND I AM MIRANDA, GOOD PRINCE.
SEEING THAT THE TWO YOUNG PEOPLE COULD EASILY FALL IN LOVE, PROSPERO WANTED TO TEST THE PRINCE.
DO NOT BELIEVE HIM MY DAUGHTER! THIS MAN SAYS HE IS OF ROYAL BLOOD,** BUT I THINK HE'S A SPY!

* clean-cut, honest, and kind-looking

** belonging to the family of a king

HE WANTS TO TAKE THE ISLAND FROM ME SO HE CAN RULE IT INSTEAD!
YOU HAVE INSULTED* ME, SIR. PREPARE TO DEFEND YOURSELF.
PROSPERO QUICKLY PUT A SPELL** OVER FERDINAND. THE PRINCE STOPPED IN HIS TRACKS.
OH, FATHER, HE CANNOT BE A SPY. HE IS SO HANDSOME!
YOU DON'T KNOW ANYTHING ABOUT HIM, MIRANDA.
SEE, HE KNOWS HE'S WRONG, AND HE CANNOT FIGHT.

* said something evil to someone

** worked magic

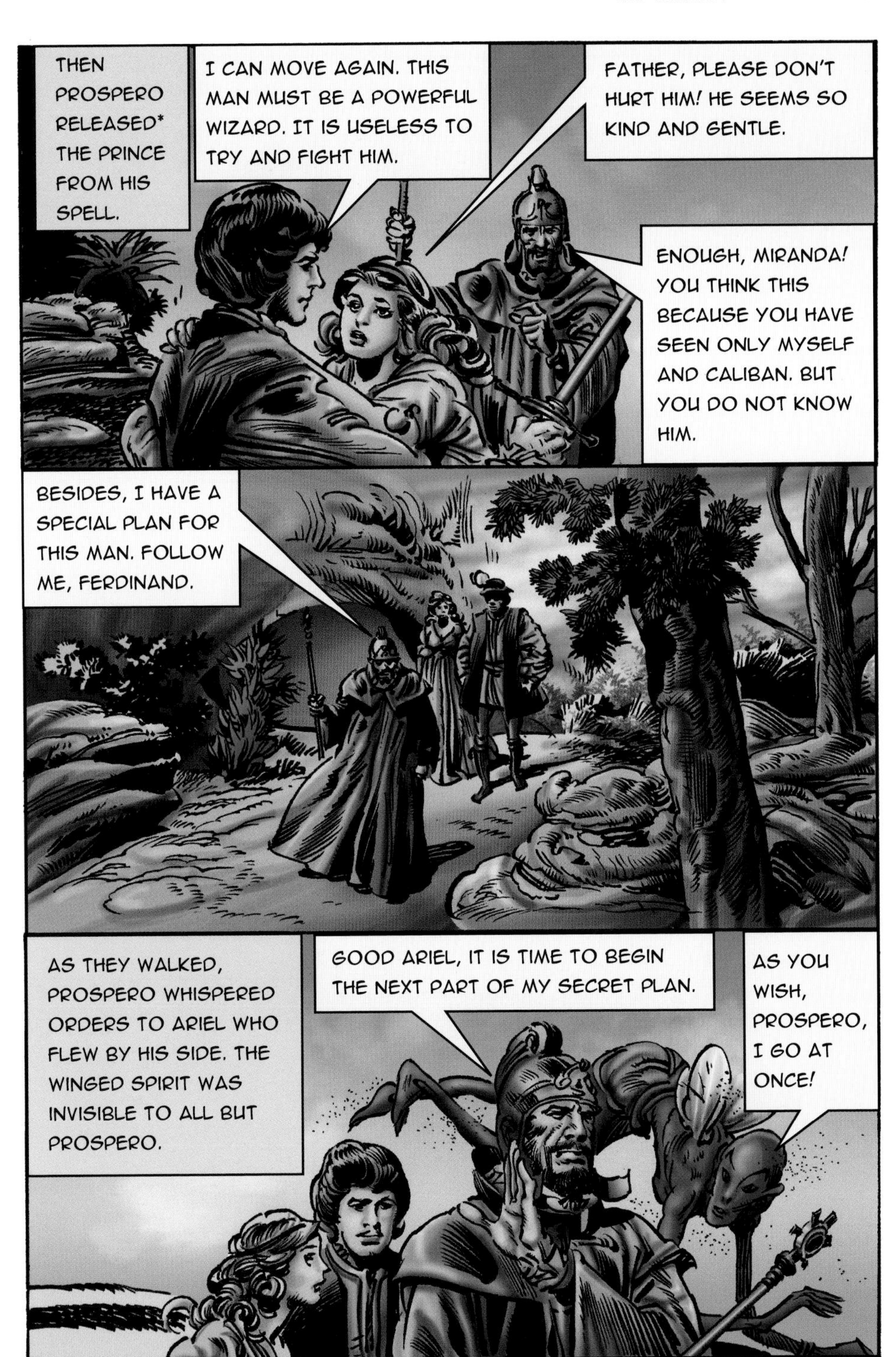
THEN PROSPERO RELEASED* THE PRINCE FROM HIS SPELL.
I CAN MOVE AGAIN. THIS MAN MUST BE A POWERFUL WIZARD. IT IS USELESS TO TRY AND FIGHT HIM.
FATHER, PLEASE DON'T HURT HIM! HE SEEMS SO KIND AND GENTLE.
ENOUGH, MIRANDA! YOU THINK THIS BECAUSE YOU HAVE SEEN ONLY MYSELF AND CALIBAN. BUT YOU DO NOT KNOW HIM.
BESIDES, I HAVE A SPECIAL PLAN FOR THIS MAN. FOLLOW ME, FERDINAND.
AS THEY WALKED, PROSPERO WHISPERED ORDERS TO ARIEL WHO FLEW BY HIS SIDE. THE WINGED SPIRIT WAS INVISIBLE TO ALL BUT PROSPERO.
GOOD ARIEL, IT IS TIME TO BEGIN THE NEXT PART OF MY SECRET PLAN.
AS YOU WISH, PROSPERO, I GO AT ONCE!

* let go

MEANWHILE, ON ANOTHER PART OF THE ISLAND, ANTONIO AND SEBASTIAN WERE THANKING THEIR LUCKY STARS TO BE ALIVE.
YOU KNOW, SEBASTIAN, IT IS A MIRACLE* WE WERE ABLE TO SWIM TO SHORE.
YES, ANTONIO. I THOUGHT WE WOULD DIE ON THAT SINKING SHIP.
BUT KING ALONSO, WHO CAME ASHORE WITH GONZALO, COULD ONLY WEEP.
MY SON FERDI-NAND IS NO-WHERE TO BE FOUND. HE MUST HAVE DROWNED TRYING TO SWIM TO SHORE.

THEN ONE OF THE NOBLES, FRANCISCO, WALKED OVER TO THE KING.

SIR, THERE IS YET A CHANCE YOUNG FERDINAND MIGHT BE ALIVE.

* something wonderful

HOW CAN YOU SAY SUCH A THING, FRANCISCO?

BECAUSE I SAW HIM SWIMMING NEAR ME FOR A TIME. HE WAS MAKING GOOD HEADWAY* AGAINST THE WAVES.

AS FRANCISCO WAS SPEAKING, GONZALO SUDDENLY REALIZED SOMETHING. SURPRISED, HE DREW NEARER TO ALONSO, HOLDING OUT HIS ARM.

THERE IS MORE CAUSE FOR HOPE, MY KING. LOOK! OUR CLOTHES ARE COMPLETELY DRY!

THERE MUST BE SOME STRONG MAGIC AT WORK ON THIS ISLAND. PERHAPS THE SAME SORCERY** THAT BROUGHT US HERE ALSO SAVED FERDINAND!

JUST THEN ARIEL FLEW BY, PLAYING SLEEPY MUSIC. ALONSO AND GONZALO YAWNED AND STRETCHED.
ALL OF A SUDDEN I AM VERY TIRED.
SO AM I. MY EYES CAN HARDLY STAY OPEN.
THEN SLEEP, MY KING. SEBASTIAN AND I WILL GUARD YOU.

* moving forward well and quickly

ARIEL WAS INVISIBLE AS GONZALO AND THE KING FELL ASLEEP ON THE BEACH. HIS MAGIC FLUTE, HOWEVER, DID NOT URGE ANTONIO OR SEBASTIAN TO REST.
WE MUST STRIKE NOW, SEBASTIAN.
WHAT DO YOU MEAN, ANTONIO?

FERDINAND IS CERTAINLY DEAD. ALONSO HAS NO SON TO TAKE HIS PLACE. IF WE KILL THE KING, YOU COULD BECOME THE *NEXT* RULER OF NAPLES!

YES, YOU ARE RIGHT! TOGETHER WE WILL SHARE MORE POWER BETWEEN US THAN EVER!
YOU STRIKE GONZALO, AND I WILL TAKE CARE OF ALONSO MYSELF!

LET US HURRY AND BE DONE WITH THIS BEFORE THE OTHERS WAKE UP.
BUT WINGED ARIEL WHISPERED A WARNING INTO THE SLEEPING ADVISOR'S EAR.
AWAKE! AWAKE, GONZALO! YOU AND THE KING ARE IN DANGER!
MAY GOOD ANGELS KEEP OUR KING SAFE.
AT THIS, KING ALONSO AWOKE.
WHAT HAS HAPPENED? ANTONIO AND SEBASTIAN— WHY ARE YOUR SWORDS DRAWN?*

* ready to be used

WHY, BROTH-ER, WE HEARD THE ROAR OF WILD ANIMALS COMING FROM THE JUNGLE.
THAT IS TRUE! WE DREW OUR SWORDS TO DEFEND YOU FROM THE BEASTS.

DID YOU HEAR ANYTHING, GONZALO?
I HEARD A STRANGE HUMMING IN MY EAR, SIR. WHEN I AWOKE, ANTONIO AND SEBASTIAN WERE STANDING AS YOU SEE THEM NOW.

THESE ARE STRANGE THINGS INDEED. LET US SEARCH THE JUNGLE FOR MY SON.
MAY HE BE SAFE FROM THE WILD BEASTS! I AM SURE HE IS SOME-WHERE ON THIS ISLAND.

HAVING DONE HIS JOB, ARIEL FLEW BACK TO REPORT TO PROSPERO.

MEANWHILE, CALIBAN WALKED ALONG A DIFFERENT PART OF THE BEACH COLLECTING FIREWOOD.
I HATE WORKING FOR PROSPERO! THE SPIRITS HE COMMANDS ARE ALWAYS AFTER ME, BITING AND HISSING!

AT THAT MOMENT, TRINCULO, THE KING'S JESTER,* CAME STUMBLING ALONG THE SAME BEACH. HE HAD JUST ESCAPED FROM THE WRECKED SHIP.

* clown

SUDDENLY, CALIBAN SAW THE JESTER DRESSED IN HIS CAP AND BELLS AND BECAME AFRAID. THE ONLY OTHER MAN HE HAD EVER SEEN BEFORE WAS PROSPERO.
THIS MUST BE ANOTHER SPIRIT PROSPERO HAS SENT!
SHAKING WITH FEAR, CALIBAN FELL TO THE GROUND AND THREW HIS CLOAK OVER HIS HEAD.
IF I HIDE, HE MAY NOT SEE ME.

JUST THEN TRINCULO CAUGHT SIGHT OF CALIBAN.
WHAT IS THIS WITH ITS FACE BURIED IN THE SAND—A MAN OR A FISH? IT CERTAINLY *SMELLS* LIKE A FISH.

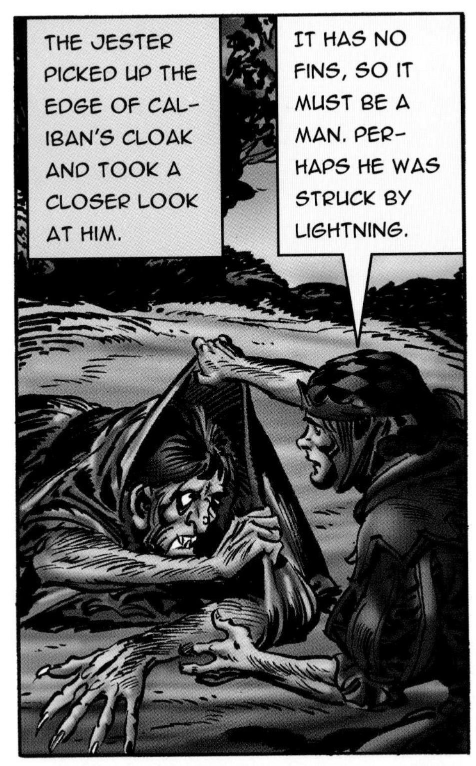
THE JESTER PICKED UP THE EDGE OF CAL-IBAN'S CLOAK AND TOOK A CLOSER LOOK AT HIM.
IT HAS NO FINS, SO IT MUST BE A MAN. PER-HAPS HE WAS STRUCK BY LIGHTNING.

JUST THEN, MORE STORM CLOUDS GATHERED OVERHEAD, AND THUNDER BOOMED.
OH, MY. IT LOOKS LIKE IT'S GOING TO RAIN AGAIN.

I HATE GETTING WET. I HOPE HIS MAN DOES NOT MIND SHARING HIS CAPE WITH ME.

A FEW MOMENTS LATER, STEPHANO, KING ALONSO'S BUTLER,* STAGGERED ALONG THE BEACH FOLLOWING TRINCULO'S FOOTPRINTS.
HIO!

WHEN HE WAS WASHED ASHORE, HE HAD FOUND A BIG JUG OF WINE NEXT TO HIM ON THE BEACH.

STEPHANO HAD BEEN DRINKING, AND HE COULD NO LONGER THINK CLEARLY.
OH! WHAT IS THIS—A MONSTER WITH FOUR LEGS AND TWO HEADS? NEVER HAVE I SEEN ONE LIKE IT BEFORE.

* serving man

I MUST CAPTURE THIS BEAST AND GIVE IT TO KING ALONSO AS A PET!
UNDER HIS CAPE, CALIBAN SHOOK ALL OVER AT THE SOUND OF STEPHANO'S THREAT.*
OH, DO NOT HARM ME, PLEASE! I'LL WORK HARDER, I PROMISE!
WHAT? A MONSTER THAT KNOWS MY LANGUAGE? I MUST GIVE HIM SOME WINE. OPEN YOUR MOUTH, MON-STER!

* warning of a planned action

JUST THEN, FROM UNDER HIS SIDE OF CALIBAN'S CAPE, TRINCULO RECOGNIZED* STEPHANO'S VOICE.
THAT SOUNDS LIKE STEPHANO. BUT NO, HE IS DROWNED, AND THIS MUST BE A DEVIL, COMING TO GET ME. HELP! HELP!
WHAT? ANOTHER VOICE FROM THE MONSTER? I WILL GIVE HIM SOME WINE IN THIS MOUTH TOO!
WAIT—YOU *ARE* STEPHANO! STEPHANO, I AM NOT A MONSTER. I AM YOUR FRIEND TRINCULO, AND WE ARE BOTH SAVED FROM THE STORM!

AT THIS, CALIBAN SAT UP AND WATCHED AS THE TWO MEN DRANK AND LAUGHED TOGETHER.
HA! HA! WE SCARED EACH OTHER WELL, DIDN'T WE, TRINCULO? THIS CALLS FOR A DRINK!
WHAT IS THAT RED JUICE? IT TASTED GOOD WHEN THEY GAVE SOME TO ME BEFORE.

* understood something from seeing or hearing it again

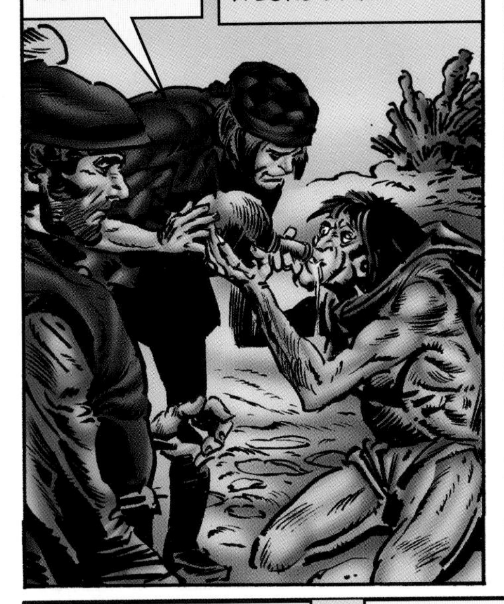
HELLO AGAIN, MONSTER. HAVE SOME MORE WINE.
JUST THEN TRINCULO PASSED THE JUG TO CALIBAN, WHO TOOK A LONG DRINK.

CALIBAN WONDERED HOW TRINCULO AND STEPHANO HAD REACHED PROSPERO'S ISLAND.
THESE MEN MUST BE GODS WHO DROPPED DOWN FROM HEAVEN. I WILL SERVE THEM INSTEAD OF PROSPERO!

BRAVE SIR, PLEASE BE MY MASTER! I'LL BRING YOU FISH, AND BERRIES, AND NUTS. I'LL SHOW YOU WHERE GOOD APPLES GROW.
SUCH A STRANGE MONSTER! BUT SINCE THE KING AND ALL THE REST ARE DEAD, WE MAY AS WELL GO WITH HIM, EH, TRINCULO?
A *STRANGE* MONSTER! A *DRUNKEN** MONSTER!

* having had too much to drink

MEANWHILE, MANY MILES AWAY FROM THE BEACH, PROSPERO HAD TAKEN FERDINAND TO A CLEARING A SHORT DISTANCE* FROM HIS CAVE. THERE, THOUSANDS OF LOGS WERE PILED IN A HUGE HEAP.
YOU MUST WORK TO EARN YOUR KEEP. I WANT YOU TO CARRY THESE LOGS TO MY CAVE AND STACK THEM NEATLY INSIDE.

* a measure of space or length

THEN PROSPERO LEFT. THE PRINCE WAS NOT USED TO SUCH WORK, AND THE TASK WAS HARD FOR HIM.
IT BREAKS MY HEART TO SEE YOU DO THIS, FERDINAND.
I DO NOT MIND, MIRANDA, AS LONG AS I HAVE A CHANCE TO BE WITH YOU.

SECRETLY WATCHING THE YOUNG PEOPLE, PROSPERO GRINNED TO HIMSELF.
THEY'RE FALL-ING IN LOVE, NO DOUBT* ABOUT IT!

IF FERDINAND WILL DO WHATEVER I ORDER JUST TO STAY CLOSE TO HER, I WILL KNOW HIS LOVE FOR MY DAUGHTER IS TRUE.

* not to know something, be uncertain

AS HE WORKED, FERDINAND'S HEART ACHED, AND HE STOPPED FOR A MOMENT TO TELL MIRANDA OF HIS FEELINGS.
MIRANDA! IF I EVER GET OFF THIS ISLAND, WILL YOU MARRY ME?

DO YOU LOVE ME, PRINCE?
WITH ALL MY HEART.

THEN I SHALL WED YOU, AND WE WILL LIVE TOGETHER FOREVER!

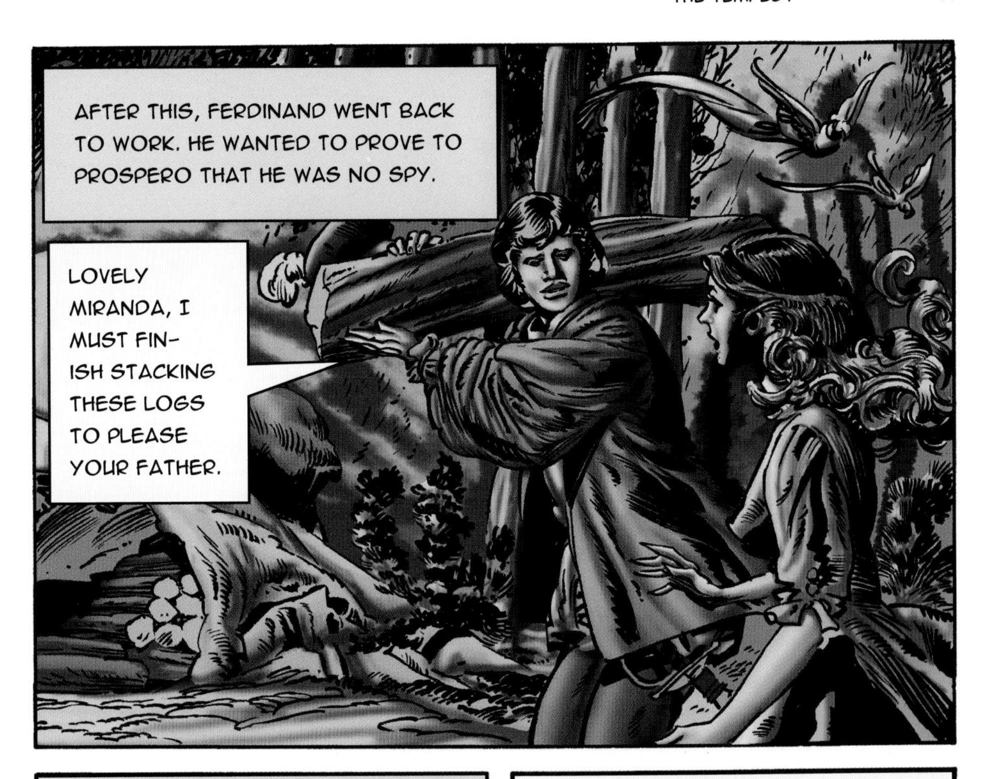
AFTER THIS, FERDINAND WENT BACK TO WORK. HE WANTED TO PROVE TO PROSPERO THAT HE WAS NO SPY.
LOVELY MIRANDA, I MUST FINISH STACKING THESE LOGS TO PLEASE YOUR FATHER.

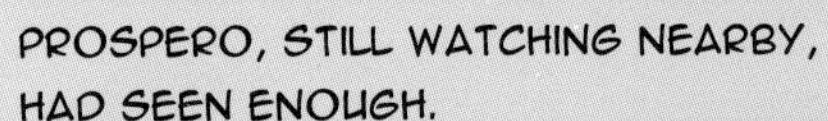
PROSPERO, STILL WATCHING NEARBY, HAD SEEN ENOUGH.

ALL GOES WELL. THOSE TWO ARE DEEPLY IN LOVE, AND I AM GLAD TO SEE IT.

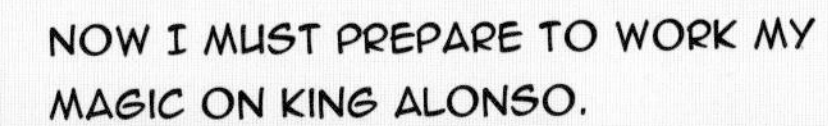
NOW I MUST PREPARE TO WORK MY MAGIC ON KING ALONSO.

MEANWHILE, CALIBAN WAS LEADING THE JESTER AND THE BUTLER THROUGH THE JUNGLE. ALL THREE CONTINUED TO DRINK FROM THE WINE JUG.
I TELL YOU, MY FORMER MASTER, PROSPERO, IS A TYRANT.* HE HAS A CAVE FULL OF GOOD THINGS, AS WELL AS A BEAUTIFUL DAUGHTER.
WHAT DOES THAT HAVE TO DO WITH US?
HELP ME KILL PROS-PERO, MASTER! THEN THE GIRL AND THIS WHOLE ISLAND WILL BE YOURS.

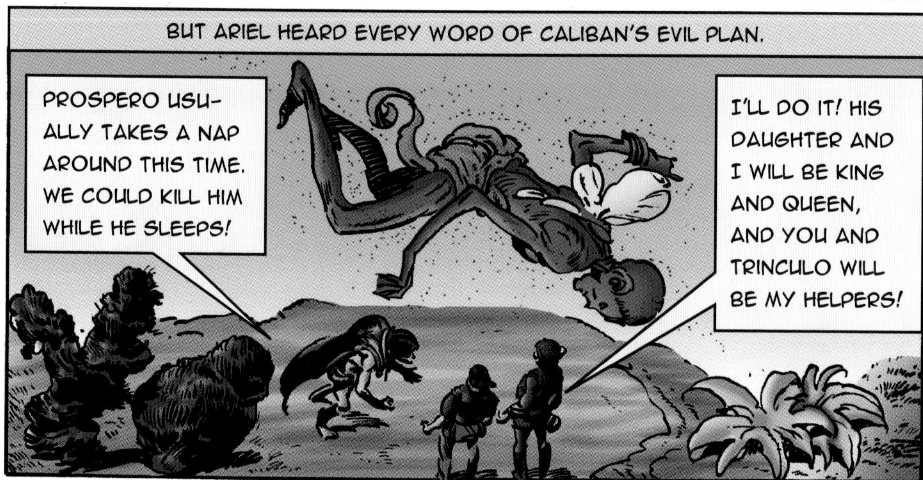
BUT ARIEL HEARD EVERY WORD OF CALIBAN'S EVIL PLAN.
PROSPERO USU-ALLY TAKES A NAP AROUND THIS TIME. WE COULD KILL HIM WHILE HE SLEEPS!
I'LL DO IT! HIS DAUGHTER AND I WILL BE KING AND QUEEN, AND YOU AND TRINCULO WILL BE MY HELPERS!

* harsh ruler

I MUST STOP CALIBAN FROM MURDERING PROSPERO. A LITTLE MUSIC WILL GET THEM TO FOLLOW ME.
EH? WHAT IS THAT MUSIC? WHERE IS IT COMING FROM?

THIS ISLAND IS FILLED WITH MANY STRANGE SPIRITS.
I BELIEVE YOU! LET'S FOLLOW IT, AND DO OUR JOB AFTERWARD.
YES, WE'LL DO THAT.

WITHOUT WATCHING WHERE THEY WERE GOING, CALIBAN AND THE TWO MEN RAN INTO A SWAMPY POOL OF WATER. THEIR FEET SANK IN ITS MUDDY BOTTOM.
WE'RE STUCK! WE CANNOT MOVE!

LEAVING THEM IN THE MUD, ARIEL FLEW BACK AND TOLD PROSPERO OF CALIBAN'S PLAN.
YOU DID THE RIGHT THING INDEED, ARIEL. BUT COME, WE MUST NOW PREPARE A BANQUET FOR THE KING OF NAPLES.
PROSPERO RAISED HIS STAFF, AND BOTH HE AND ARIEL DISAPPEARED INTO THE AIR.
THE TRAVELERS MUST NOT SEE ME YET, SO I MUST BECOME INVISIBLE.
AT THAT SAME MOMENT, ALONSO, GONZALO, ANTONIO AND SEBASTIAN WERE MAKING THEIR WAY THROUGH THE THICK JUNGLE, STILL SEARCHING FOR FERDINAND.
ALONSO AND GONZALO ARE BOTH VERY TIRED. WE MUST KILL THEM TONIGHT WHEN THEY WILL BE TOO WEAK TO FIGHT BACK.
YES. WE WILL DO IT TONIGHT.

* a great feast

JUST THEN THE MEN WALKED INTO A CLEARING WHERE A TABLE WAS SET FOR A FEAST. PROSPERO REMAINED INVISIBLE AND WATCHED WHAT ALONSO WOULD DO.
WHAT? THIS IS A FEAST FIT FOR A KING! LET US EAT!

SUDDENLY, ARIEL APPEARED ON THE TABLE. PROSPERO'S MAGIC HAD CHANGED HIM SO THE KINDLY SPIRIT LOOKED LIKE A DEMON.*
THREE OF YOU MEN HAVE SINFUL HEARTS!

* devil, evil spirit

YOU MUST BE PUNISHED—ES-PECIALLY* KING ALONSO WHO TOOK MILAN'S THRONE FROM GOOD PROSPERO!
OH, NO!

WITH THAT, ARIEL CLAPPED HIS WINGS AND THE FEAST WAS GONE.

SUDDENLY ALONSO FELT VERY SORRY FOR WHAT HE HAD DONE. HE FELL TO HIS KNEES.
NOW I KNOW WHY FERDINAND DROWNED. HE WAS TAKEN FROM ME BECAUSE OF WHAT I ONCE DID TO PROSPERO.

I REGRET** WHAT I DID TO PROSPERO. PERHAPS I SHOULD DROWN MYSELF TOO!

*mostly

** felt sorry

LEAVING ALONSO TO HIS THOUGHTS, PROSPERO AND ARIEL RETURNED AT ONCE TO PROSPERO'S CAVE.
ALONSO SEEMS REALLY SORRY FOR WHAT HE DID TO YOU.
YES, ARIEL. NOW I WANT YOU TO BRING SOME OTHER SPIRITS HERE. THEY MUST BLESS THE LOVE OF FER-DINAND AND MIRANDA.

ARIEL LEFT, AND PROSPERO WENT TO SEE THE YOUNG PRINCE OF NAPLES WHO WAS STILL HARD AT WORK.

FERDINAND! YOU MUST FORGIVE WHAT I HAVE DONE TO YOU! I ALWAYS KNEW YOU WERE NOT A SPY.

BUT I HAD TO BE SURE YOUR LOVE FOR MY DAUGHTER WAS REAL. SO I DECIDED TO TEST YOU WITH HARD WORK.

NOW I AM SATISFIED.* YOU MAY MARRY MIRANDA.
I SHALL CARE FOR HER ALWAYS!

I AM GLAD. NOW ARIEL IS PREPARING A PARTY FOR US. THE SPIRITS WILL COME TO BLESS YOUR LOVE!

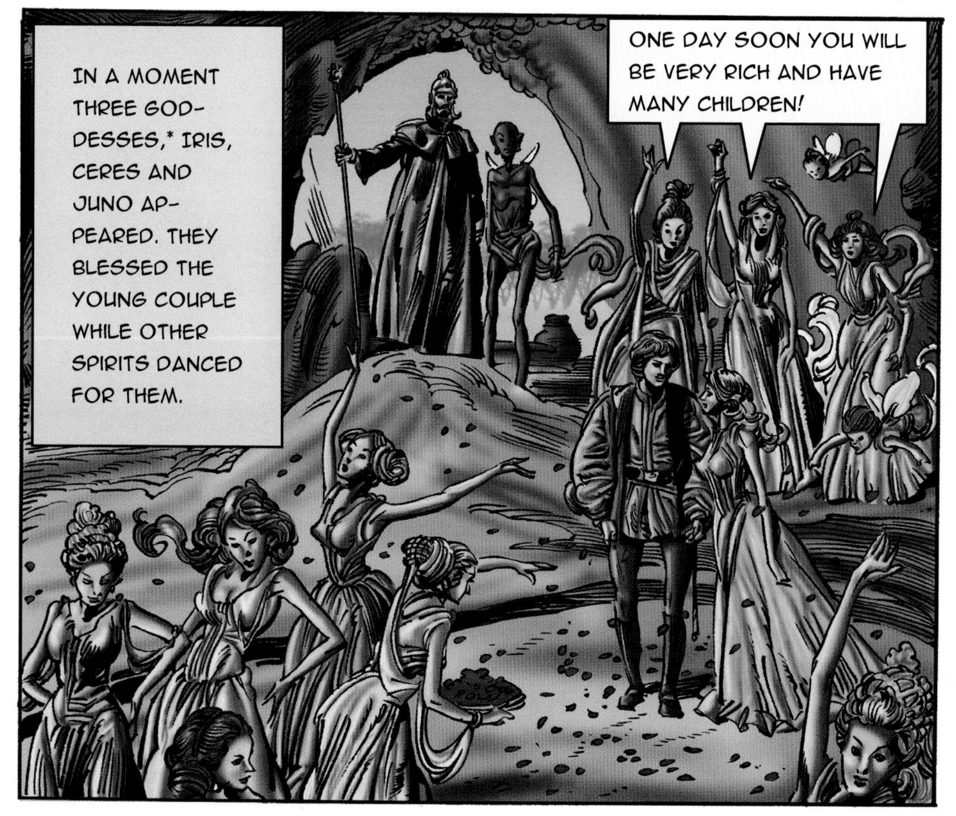
IN A MOMENT THREE GOD-DESSES,* IRIS, CERES AND JUNO AP-PEARED. THEY BLESSED THE YOUNG COUPLE WHILE OTHER SPIRITS DANCED FOR THEM.
ONE DAY SOON YOU WILL BE VERY RICH AND HAVE MANY CHILDREN!

* happy that something worked out well

** female spirits who have power over various parts of men's lives

AS THE SPIR-
ITS DANCED,
PROSPERO
SUDDENLY
REMEMBERED
CALIBAN.
ARIEL, WE MUST DO SOMETHING ABOUT THAT MONSTER AND THE TWO MEN HE MET.

THAT IS ENOUGH! SPIRITS, LEAVE US! I HAVE WORK TO DO.

WHAT HAS UPSET YOUR FATHER, MY LOVE?
I DON'T KNOW, FERDINAND. HE IS VERY ANGRY.

IN A MOMENT PROSPERO HAD DECIDED WHAT TO DO.
ARIEL, HANG A LINE OF BEAUTIFUL CLOTHES IN FRONT OF MY DOOR. THEY WILL ACT AS BAIT* FOR CALIBAN.
HAVING DONE THAT, ARIEL FLEW BACK TO THE BLACK POOL OF WATER AND SET CALIBAN AND THE TWO MEN FREE.
WE CAN MOVE AGAIN.
CALIBAN TOOK STEPHANO AND TRINCULO TO PROSPERO'S VERY DOORSTEP.
THERE IS THE WIZARD'S HOME. GO INSIDE AND KILL HIM!

* something that will tempt someone to take it

BUT STEPHANO AND TRINCULO WOULD GO NO FURTHER. THEY WANTED TO STEAL THE CLOTHES HANGING ON PROSPERO'S LINE.
THESE CLOTHES ARE WORTH A FORTUNE!
DON'T STOP, FRIENDS. WE MUST KILL PROSPERO BEFORE HE FINDS OUT ABOUT US!
BUT IT WAS ALREADY TOO LATE. PROSPERO SENT SOME SPIRITS IN THE SHAPE OF HUNTING DOGS TO CHASE THEM AWAY.
SILVER, MOUNTAIN, FURY, TYRANT! AFTER THEM!
THESE HOUNDS ARE DEVILS!
THIS IS PROSPERO'S MAGIC. HE IS TOO STRONG TO FIGHT AGAINST!

NOW EVERYTHING IS GOING AS I PLANNED!

ARIEL! GO TO THE WOODS WHERE WE LEFT ALONSO AND THE OTHERS. BRING THEM HERE TO ME.

QUICK AS A WINK, THE WINGED SPIRIT CAME BACK WITH THE SIX MEN. NONE OF THEM RECOGNIZED PROSPERO AS THE OLD DUKE OF MILAN.

WHO ARE YOU, WIZARD? AND WHY HAVE YOU BROUGHT US HERE?
YOU DO NOT KNOW WHO I AM? THEN LOOK HERE!

AS PROSPERO RAISED HIS STAFF, ARIEL DRESSED HIM IN THE GARMENTS HE USED TO WEAR AS DUKE OF MILAN. ALONSO GASPED IN DISBELIEF.*
PROSPERO!

FORGIVE ME, PROSPERO. I HAVE SINNED AGAINST YOU.
I SENSE YOU HAVE LEARNED YOUR LESSON AND SPEAK THE TRUTH, ALONSO. I FORGIVE YOU.

THE GOOD GONZALO COULD HARDLY BELIEVE HIS EYES.
I AM HAPPY TO SEE YOU ALIVE, PROSPERO.
I HAVE YOU TO THANK FOR THAT, MY FRIEND.

* thinking that something is not true

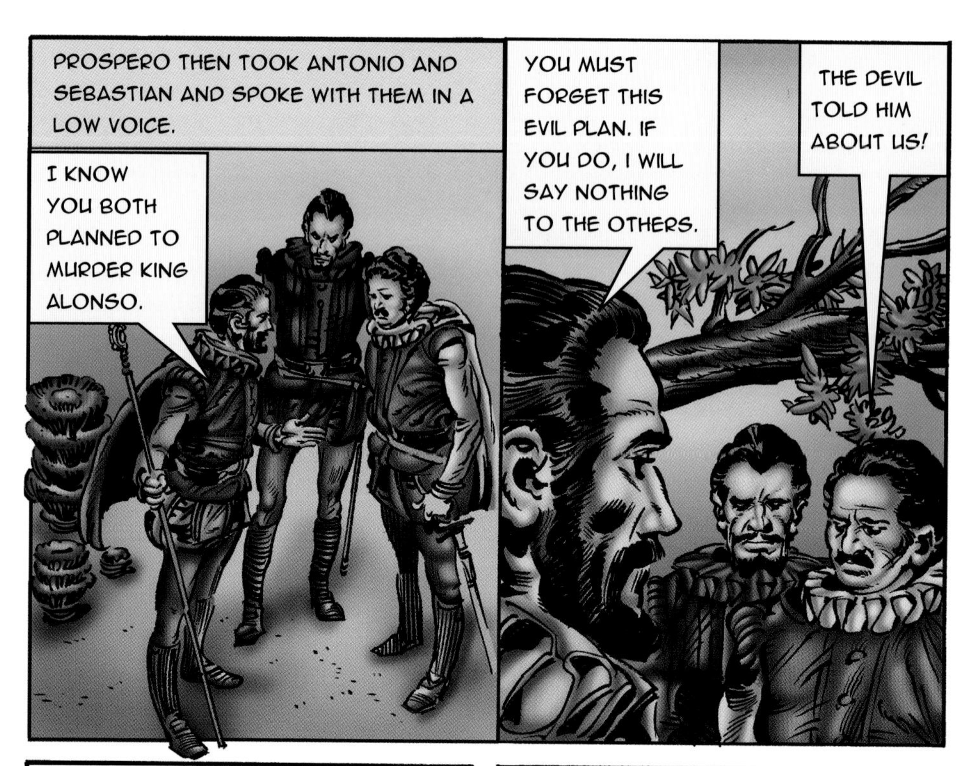
PROSPERO THEN TOOK ANTONIO AND SEBASTIAN AND SPOKE WITH THEM IN A LOW VOICE.
I KNOW YOU BOTH PLANNED TO MURDER KING ALONSO.
YOU MUST FORGET THIS EVIL PLAN. IF YOU DO, I WILL SAY NOTHING TO THE OTHERS.
THE DEVIL TOLD HIM ABOUT US!

NO, NOT THE DEVIL, SEBASTIAN. BUT YOU AND MY BROTHER ANTONIO MUST RETURN MY THRONE TO ME, OR YOU WILL SEE WHAT MY MAGIC CAN DO!

I WILL, MY BROTHER. IT IS YOURS AGAIN.
THEN I FORGIVE YOU, ANTONIO.

BUT EVEN THOUGH PROSPERO HAD FORGIVEN HIM, ALONSO WAS STILL SAD, BELIEVING THAT HIS SON WAS DEAD.
I'VE LOST MY SON, PROSPERO. I WILL NEVER BE HAPPY AGAIN.

YES YOU WILL, ALONSO. LOOK HERE!
FERDINAND! AND A LOVELY GIRL AS WELL.
FATHER, YOU ARE SAFE! THIS IS INDEED A HAPPY DAY!

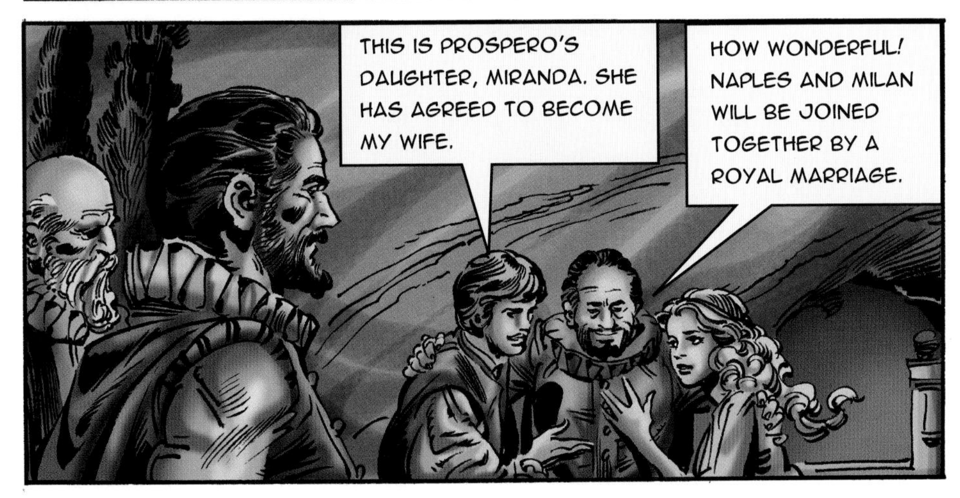
THIS IS PROSPERO'S DAUGHTER, MIRANDA. SHE HAS AGREED TO BECOME MY WIFE.
HOW WONDERFUL! NAPLES AND MILAN WILL BE JOINED TOGETHER BY A ROYAL MARRIAGE.

JUST THEN ARIEL CAME BUZZING IN, FOLLOWED BY CALIBAN, STEPHANO, AND TRINCULO.
I AM SORRY I TRIED TO HURT YOU, PROSPERO. NEVER AGAIN WILL I DO SUCH A THING.
FOR ONCE I BELIEVE YOU, CALIBAN. NOW GO, AND PREPARE A PLACE FOR THESE VISITORS.
THE JESTER AND I WERE DRUNK, SIR. PLEASE DO NOT JUDGE US HARSHLY.
I UNDERSTAND, AND I FORGIVE YOU BOTH.

NOW, MY FRIENDS, COME AND JOIN ME FOR MY LAST NIGHT ON THIS ISLAND. I WILL TELL YOU MY STORY, AND TOMORROW WE SHALL SET SAIL FOR ITALY IN YOUR SHIP, WHICH I HAVE KEPT SAFE.

MANY MILES AWAY, THE SLEEPING SAILORS SUDDENLY AWOKE AND GOT THE SHIP READY FOR SAILING.

MASTER PROSPERO. . . !
I HAVE NOT FORGOTTEN YOU, GOOD ARIEL. YOU ARE NOW FREE. FAREWELL!

AT LAST ALL IS WELL, AND I HAVE NO MORE NEED OF MAGIC. FROM NOW ON I WILL RULE MY PEOPLE BY LAWS OF MAN, AND I WILL DO IT WITH A GOOD HEART!
THE END